The Thinking Place

The Thinking Place

by BARBARA M. JOOSSE

Pictures by Kay Chorao

ALFRED A. KNOPF   NEW YORK

THIS IS A BORZOI BOOK
PUBLISHED BY ALFRED A. KNOPF, INC.

Library of Congress Cataloging in Publication Data

Joosse, Barbara M.
   The thinking place.

   SUMMARY: Whenever she's been naughty, Elisabeth
must spend time in the thinking place.
   [1. Behavior—Fiction] I. Chorao, Kay. II. Title.
PZ7.J7435Th   [E]   81-515
ISBN 0-394-84908-6   AACR1
ISBN 0-394-94908-0 (lib. bdg.)
             10 9 8 7 6 5 4 3 2 1

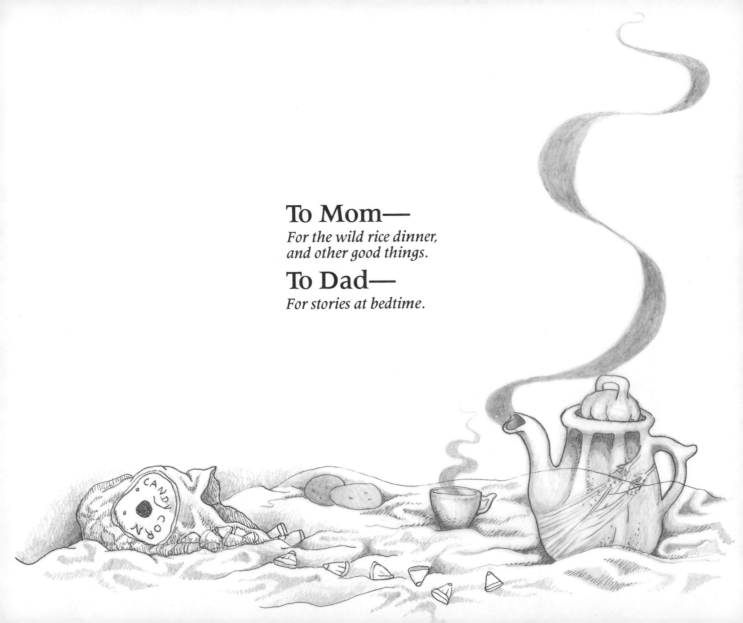

To Mom—
*For the wild rice dinner,
and other good things.*

To Dad—
For stories at bedtime.

 am sitting in the thinking place.

The thinking place is where Mama sends me when I am naughty. If I spill my lemonade and it is not an accident, Mama sends me to the thinking place. If I pound on the furniture with my tool set, Mama sends me to the thinking place.

I go to the thinking place, Mama says, to think about what I did. I go to the thinking place, Mama says, to be sorry for what I did. When I've thought about it, and when I am *really* sorry, I can leave.

I'm in the thinking place now because I put candy corn in the dishwasher. But I'm not sorry. Nobody ever said, "Elisabeth, don't put candy corn in the dishwasher." So how could I know?

I am not sorry I did it, but I am sorry I'm here. There is nothing to do. There is nothing to see.

This is boring boring boring.

Here comes my friend Melissa. She is very beautiful, with long blond hair, and she wears fancy dresses.

Mama always says Melissa is not really here, just in my imagination. But Mama is never in the thinking place when Melissa comes.

Melissa is carrying a tray with a china tea set and cookies. We chat for a while, and then Melissa offers me tea.

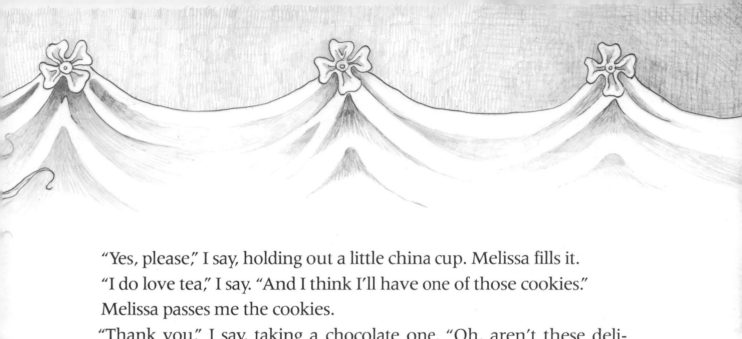

"Yes, please," I say, holding out a little china cup. Melissa fills it.

"I do love tea," I say. "And I think I'll have one of those cookies."

Melissa passes me the cookies.

"Thank you," I say, taking a chocolate one. "Oh, aren't these delicious? Maybe I'll have two."

"Elisabeth? Elisabeth!" calls Mama. I think she has been calling me for a very long time.

"What?" I say.

Mama says, "You are supposed to be thinking quietly. You are supposed to be thinking about the candy corn."

Candy corn. I thought it would be fun when I put it in. But then when Mama turned on the dishwasher there was an awful noise and smoke came out. The dishwasher was like a horrible monster.

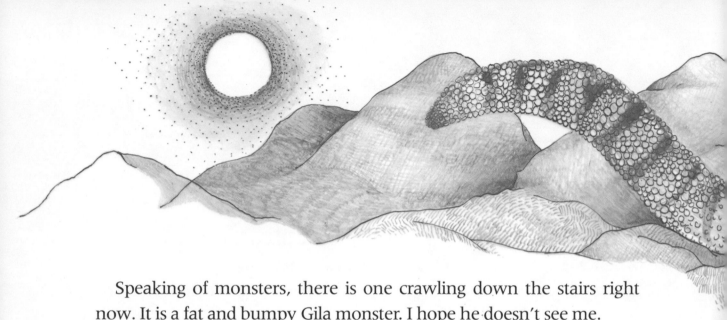

Speaking of monsters, there is one crawling down the stairs right now. It is a fat and bumpy Gila monster. I hope he doesn't see me.

He sees me.

I can tell because he is sticking out his tongue. When a Gila monster does that, he is tasting the air to see where his food is hiding.

And I am his food!

I run down the stairs as fast as I can. There's Mama. I hold on to her legs very tight. She gives me a little hug. Then she takes me back to the thinking place.

"You haven't finished thinking, Elisabeth," she says.

Thinking. What I think is that this place is terrible. What I think is that I don't want to be here.

And I think that Mama is very upset.

First Mama was mad when she saw the smoke coming out of the dishwasher. Then she was sad when she called the repairman.

It took him a long time to fix the dishwasher.

I wonder if the repairman could fix my felt markers. A witch pulled out the colored parts so they don't write anymore.

I think I hear that witch right now.
Whissa-whissa-whissa-whissa.
That witch will try to get me in trouble. I wonder what she will do this time.

She will probably throw all my toys out of the toy box, or put chewed-up bubble gum under my pillow.

Maybe she will do something worse, like writing "Elisabeth" with lipstick all over the wall next to my bed! I was thinking of doing that this morning.

Now that witch is in the bathroom, opening up Mama's make-up case. She is getting out the lipstick.

She is going into my bedroom, and now she is climbing on my bed.

ELISA͞TH

"Mama, Mama!" I yell.

Mama comes back.

"Mama," I say, "I'm sorry. I'm sorry I put candy corn in the dishwasher and I'm sorry it made a mess and I'm sorry you had to have it fixed."

"OK, Elisabeth," says Mama. "I'm sure you won't do it again. You can leave now."

"And *I* wouldn't write 'Elisabeth' on the wall with lipstick," I say as I run up the stairs.

I hope that witch didn't write on the wall. It would be a mess and Mama would have to call the repairman to paint the wall.

I open the door.

There is Mama's lipstick.

But there is nothing on the wall. I must have scared the witch away before she could get me in trouble.

I'm safe!

Now I think I will stand on my bed and pretend the rug is the ocean and there are wild sharks waiting to get me.

But before I do, I am going to put this lipstick away.

Barbara M. Joosse (she pronounces it JOEsee) is a lifelong resident of Wisconsin. After receiving a B.A. in journalism from the University of Wisconsin, she worked as an advertising copywriter. "Then I worked as a mother," she says. "Then I wrote about it." She and her husband live in a solar house in Hartford, Wisconsin, with their two daughters, whom she describes as "my writing impediments and inspiration." *The Thinking Place* is her first book.

Kay Chorao (she pronounces it shaRO) has a B.A. in art history from Wheaton College and studied at the Chelsea School of Art in London, and the School of Visual Arts in New York. An award-winning artist, she has illustrated some thirty-five books for children. Her work has been honored by the American Institute of Graphic Arts and the Society of Illustrators. Ms. Chorao lives in New York City with her husband, who is a painter, and their three sons.